Si, Samirah

Camille Smith

ISBN 978-1-0980-8873-6 (paperback)
ISBN 978-1-0980-8874-3 (digital)

Christian Faith Publishing, Inc.
832 Park Avenue
Meadville, PA 16335
www.christianfaithpublishing.com

Printed in the United States of America

Samirah Jo

1 2 3
6
7 8 9
10 11 12
months

Mommy, can you make me waffles?

Si, Samirah.

Mommy, can I wear my yellow dress today?

Si, Samirah.

Mommy, can we go to the park?

Si, Samirah.

Mommy, can we have grilled cheese for lunch?

Si, Samirah.

Mommy, can we paint a picture?

Si, Samirah.

Mommy, can I have a hug?

Si, Samirah.

Mommy, can I have a kiss?

Si, Samirah.

Mommy, do you love me?

Si, Samirah. Always.

About the Author

Camille is a former kindergarten teacher who is now a stay-at-home mom and author. She has always had a love for children's books and, along the way, discovered a new love for creating them as well. When she's not taking care of her little butterfly Samirah, she enjoys running, learning Spanish, and traveling the world. She lives with her husband and daughter in Arlington, Texas.

9 781098 088736